SILLY SIDNEY

Written by Morgan Matthews
Illustrated by Richard Max Kolding

Troll Associates

Library of Congress Cataloging in Publication Data

Matthews, Morgan.
  Silly Sidney.

  Summary: Silly Sidney decides to keep fall from coming
by putting the leaves back on the trees.
    [1. Squirrels—Fiction. 2. Autumn—Fiction]
I. Kolding, Richard Max, ill. II. Title.
PZ7.M43425Si   1986   [E]   85-14063
ISBN 0-8167-0610-7 (lib. bdg.)
ISBN 0-8167-0611-5 (pbk.)

SILLY SIDNEY

In a big field stood an oak tree.
It was the only tree in the field.
In the oak lived a little squirrel.
His name was Sidney.

Sidney was a silly squirrel. And
he was a little lazy. He always
thought up ways to get out of
work. That's why he was called
Silly Little Sidney.

One chilly morning Sidney
woke up.
"I'll warm up in the summer
sun," he said.
Out of his hole he scooted.

BRRR! The cold wind blew.
It chilled him from top to tail.
Summer was almost over.
"Oh no! Not fall," he said.
"After fall comes winter. I do
not like fall or winter. I like
summer."

When fall comes, squirrels must work. They must find nuts. They must save nuts for winter. For in winter there are no nuts to find and eat. So squirrels must work very hard in the fall.

Lazy little Sidney did not like hard work.
"I want summer to stay," he said. "I must stop fall from coming! But how?"

Tree leaves began to fall. PLOP!
One landed on Sidney. BOING!
Sidney got a silly idea.

"Leaves!" he cried. "When leaves drop, fall comes. If leaves do not drop, fall cannot come. If fall cannot come, summer will stay! HOORAY!"

What a silly little squirrel Sidney
was! What a silly idea he had!
Summer must go. Fall must
come. Winter must come, too!
The seasons must change.

Leaves were falling. Plop! Plop!
Sidney said, "I must stop fall
from coming. I must put the
leaves back."

Sidney scooted into his hole.
He got some tacks. Then out he
went. He got a leaf. Up he went.
Silly Sidney tacked the leaf back.

Up and down. Up and down.
Up and down went Silly Little
Sidney. He tacked all the leaves
back. It took him all day.

"Now to bed," said Sidney, with
a smile. "The season cannot
change. Fall cannot come.
Summer will stay."

The next day he woke up.
He looked out. On the ground
were more leaves.
"Oh no," cried Sidney, "more
leaves and no more tacks.
What to do?"

He saw some string. It was kite
string. BOING! He got another
idea.
"I can use kite string," said
Sidney. "I can tie the leaves on
with kite string."

Down the oak tree he scooted.
WOOSH! Then back up he went.
Sidney tied leaves on. He tied
them on with kite string.

All day long he worked very
hard. He used all the kite string.
Lots of leaves were tacked or
tied. Other leaves were not
tacked or tied.

Sidney said, "This is hard work. This work is as hard as finding nuts. But I do not have to find nuts. Fall will not come. Winter will not come."
Silly Little Sidney went to bed.

What happened next? Other
leaves fell. Drop! Drop! Drop!
They fell and fell. Leaves that
were not tacked or tied fell and
fell. Fall was coming.

The next day Sidney had more
work. Leaves were on the
ground.
"How can I put them back?"
said Sidney. "I have no tacks!
I have no kite string. I need
something to put leaves back."

Silly Little Sidney looked in his hole. He looked here. He looked there. He looked everywhere. What did he find? Glue! "Glue will stick the leaves back on," said Sidney.

Glue did stick the leaves back on.
Sidney glued leaves everywhere.
No more leaves on the ground.
No more glue.

PLOP! One more leaf dropped.
"I'm too tired to get you now,"
Sidney said. "I will get you
later."
The tired little squirrel went
to bed.

When Sidney got up, warm sun
shone into his hole.
"Summer sun," cried Silly Little
Sidney. "I made summer stay.
HOORAY! Now I must go out.
I must put back that one leaf."
Out of his hole he scooted.

"Oh no!" he cried.
His fur stood up. Not one leaf
did he see. He saw lots and lots
of leaves around the oak tree.

What to do? No more tacks!
No more string! No more glue!
Sidney thought and thought.
BOING!
"I have ribbons!" Sidney said.
"Lots of ribbons! With ribbons I
can tie leaves back on."

WOOSH! He got the ribbons.
WOOSH! Down the oak he
went. He got a leaf. He tied it
on. Up and down. Up and down
all day long.

He tied ribbons here. He tied
ribbons there. He tied ribbons
everywhere. Sidney used all the
ribbons.

What a funny oak tree. What a
funny tree to see. Leaves were
tacked. Leaves were tied with
kite string. Leaves were glued.
Leaves were tied with many
ribbons.

"No more leaves can come down," Sidney said. "All the leaves are put back. Now the season will not change. It cannot change."

All the leaves were not put back.
One leaf was not. PLOP! Down
it dropped. On the ground it fell.

Sidney saw the leaf. He was out
of tacks. He was out of kite
string. He was out of glue and
ribbons. Was he out of everything?

Back to his hole he went.
He wanted something to put one
leaf back.

By his bed he found something.
"Bubble gum," he cried.
"Chewed bubble gum is sticky.
I will chew bubble gum and
make it sticky!"

Silly Sidney chewed bubble gum.
He chewed and chewed and
chewed. He chewed the bubble
gum until it was sticky.

"Now I will put back the leaf,"
said Sidney. "I will put it back
with sticky bubble gum."

Sidney got the leaf. To the top of the oak he went. With sticky bubble gum, he stuck the leaf back on.

"Now I am done," he said. "Fall
cannot come. Summer will stay.
HOORAY! Hooray for Sidney
Squirrel."

But fall did come. One day, cold
wind *wooshed* into Sidney's hole.
It woke him up.

He looked out of his hole.
"Why is it cold? How? Why?"
Sidney cried.

"Because fall has come," said an
owl.
"I stopped fall from coming,"
cried Sidney. "I put all the leaves
back."

"Silly Little Sidney," said the
owl, "putting leaves back cannot
stop fall. Seasons change.
Summer went. Fall is here.
Now what will you do?"

"I will not be silly anymore. I
will look for nuts. I will find
nuts. I will save nuts for winter,"
said Sidney.

And that is what he did!